A Note to Parents

Welcome to REAL KIDS READERS, a series of phonics-based books for children who are beginning to read. In the classroom, educators use phonics to teach children how to sound out unfamiliar words, providing a firm foundation for reading skills. At home, you can use REAL KIDS READERS to reinforce and build on that foundation, because the books follow the same basic phonic guidelines that children learn in school.

Of course the best way to help your child become a good reader is to make the experience fun—and REAL KIDS READERS do that, too. With their realistic story lines and lively characters, the books engage children's imaginations. With their clean design and sparkling photographs, they provide picture clues that help new readers decipher the text. The combination is sure to entertain young children and make them truly want to read.

REAL KIDS READERS have been developed at three distinct levels to make it easy for children to read at their own pace.

- LEVEL 1 is for children who are just beginning to read.
- LEVEL 2 is for children who can read with help.
- LEVEL 3 is for children who can read on their own.

A controlled vocabulary provides the framework at each level. Repetition, rhyme, and humor help increase word skills. Because children can understand the words and follow the stories, they quickly develop confidence. They go back to each book again and again, increasing their proficiency and sense of accomplishment, until they're ready to move on to the next level. The result is a rich and rewarding experience that will help them develop a lifelong love of reading.

With love and thanks
to Hilary Jensen Rice.
—P. J.

Produced by DWAI / Seventeenth Street Productions, Inc.

Library of Congress Cataloging-in-Publication Data

Jensen, Patsy.
    Loose-tooth Luke / by Patsy Jensen ; photography by Dorothy Handelman.
        p.   cm. — (Real kids readers. Level 3)
    Summary: When Luke and his friends find out that he is the only one who still has all his
baby teeth, everyone has a suggestion for making his one loose tooth come out.
    ISBN 0-7613-2009-1 (lib. bdg.). — ISBN 0-7613-2034-2 (pbk.)
    [1. Teeth—Fiction.] I. Handelman, Dorothy, ill. II. Title. III. Series.
PZ7.J4385Lo   1998
[Fic]—dc21   97-31371
                                                                               CIP
                                                                               AC

pbk: 10 9 8 7 6 5 4 3 2 1
lib: 10 9 8 7 6 5 4 3 2 1

Loose-Tooth Luke

Patsy Jensen
Photographs by Dorothy Handelman

M

The Millbrook Press
Brookfield, Connecticut

Luke and Max were drawing with chalk on the sidewalk in Pocket Park. The park was small, with houses on the sides. But it was just the right size for the boys and their friends.

Luke was making a dragon. He used the last bit of red chalk to draw fire coming from the dragon's mouth.

"Awesome dragon," said Max.

"Thanks," said Luke. "Your picture is good too. Only I'm not sure what it is."

Max laughed. "It's a castle," he said. "But it looks more like a stack of boxes. I guess I'm better at building things than I am at drawing them."

Just then Beth and Lisa came by.

"Hi," said Lisa. "Can we draw too?"

"Sure," said Max. "But we've used up most of the chalk." He held up a small piece to show her.

"We can buy more," said Beth. "Look what I found under my pillow this morning."

Beth opened her hand. She had four shiny quarters. "I lost my fifth tooth, so I got money from the tooth fairy."

"You've lost five teeth?" said Luke. "No fair. I haven't even lost one!"

"Really?" said Lisa. "I've lost two."

"I've lost six, and another one is loose," said Max.

All of a sudden, Luke felt weird. He was the only one who still had all his baby teeth.

"Maybe one of your teeth is loose," Lisa said kindly. "Why don't you check and see?"

"Okay," said Luke. He pushed his tongue against his top teeth. They didn't move. He pushed his tongue against his bottom teeth. One of them moved!

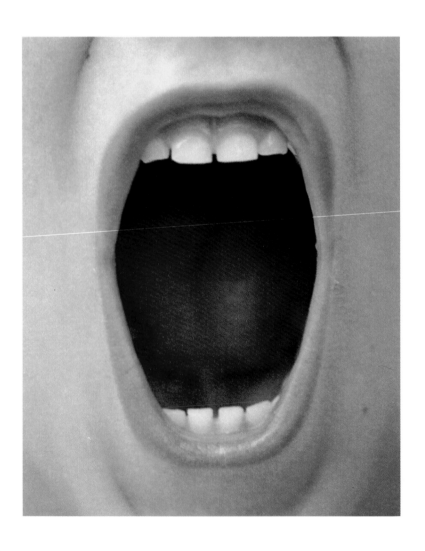

"My tooth is loose! My tooth is loose!" Luke yelled. He opened his mouth and wiggled his bottom front tooth.

"Cool!" said his friends.

Luke grinned. Finally he had a loose tooth! But then he started to worry. When would his tooth come out? Would it hang around in his mouth for years and years?

Luke's smile turned into a frown.

"Now what's wrong?" asked Beth.

Luke shrugged. "Well, I'm happy my tooth is loose. But now I wonder how I'm going to get it out."

13

"Don't worry. I know what to do," said Max. "We'll make a big machine. It will grab your loose tooth. It will wiggle it and wiggle it. Then it will yank it out—like this."
He pretended to pull Luke's tooth.

Luke's eyes got very big. "I don't know, Max," he said. "It sounds kind of—um— hard to make."

"Trust me. It will be easy," said Max. "We'll call it The World's Fastest Tooth-Pulling Machine. Every kid around Pocket Park will want to use it."

He picked up a little piece of chalk and started to draw the machine. "We'll need gears and wires and nuts and bolts. And we'll need a big, strong pincher thing to grab the tooth."

Luke looked at Max's drawing. The Tooth-Pulling Machine did not look like fun. In fact, it looked creepy. But maybe it would work.

Luke really wanted to lose a tooth.
"Okay," he said. "Let's give it a try."
"Great," said Max. "Come on, you guys.
We'll build it at Luke's house."

"No, thanks," said Beth. "I'm going to go buy more chalk."

"I'll go with you," said Lisa. "Good luck with the machine, you two. We'll meet you back here later."

The girls left the park.

"This machine will be so cool," Max said. "We'll put the motor on it. Then, *vroom!* It will pull out your tooth like that." He snapped his fingers.

Luke's tummy did a flip-flop. This machine was sounding worse and worse!

"A m-m-m-motor?" he said. "I don't think we have one."

"Rats!" said Max. "The machine won't work without a motor."

"Oh," said Luke. "That's too bad." But inside he felt much better.

The boys went to Luke's house.

"I've got an idea!" said Max. "Do you have any string?"

"Sure," said Luke. "What for?"

"You'll see," said Max.

The boys went on a string hunt. They found fat string and thin string, scratchy string and smooth string. They made kind of a mess. But Max finally found what he was looking for.

"This is just right—thin but strong," he said.

Max led the way to Luke's room. He cut a long piece of string. Then he tied one end to the doorknob.

"You sit on the chair," he said to Luke. "I'll tie the other end of the string around your tooth. Then I'll slam the door. *Bang!* The string will go tight, and your tooth will pop right out. Okay?"

"I guess," Luke said. But he didn't like this plan much better than the first one.

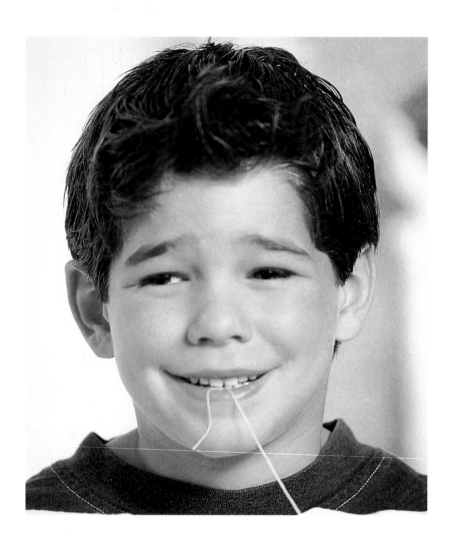

Max tied the string to Luke's tooth. "Are you ready?" he asked.

Luke gulped. "Ready," he said.

"Then here we go," said Max. He slammed the door. *Bang!*

Luke jumped as the string flew from his mouth. But his tooth stayed in place.

"Rats!" said Max. "Your tooth is very slippery. Do you want to try again?"

"That's okay," Luke said quickly. "I'm sure my tooth is too slippery. Besides, Mom hates it when I slam the door."

"Okay. I've got one more idea," said Max. "And this one won't even hurt. All you have to do is brush your teeth. That's how I lost my third tooth. I brushed it hard, and it fell right out."

The boys went to the bathroom. Luke put toothpaste on his toothbrush. He brushed and brushed. He spit into the sink. Then he brushed some more.

The tooth did not fall out.

"Try brushing harder," said Max.

Luke brushed harder. But it didn't do any good. "Now I have the cleanest teeth in town," he said. "But they are all still in my mouth."

"Too bad," said Max. "What do you want to do now?"

"Let's go back to the park," said Luke. "Beth and Lisa should be there by now. Maybe they will know what to do."

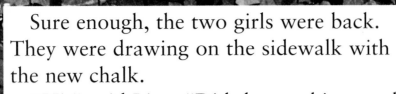

Sure enough, the two girls were back. They were drawing on the sidewalk with the new chalk.

"Hi," said Lisa. "Did the machine work? Did your tooth come out?"

"We didn't build it, and my tooth didn't come out," said Luke. He picked up a piece of white chalk. He added tiny baby teeth to his dragon's mouth. Now the dragon didn't look awesome anymore. It looked silly—just the way he felt.

"I know something that will make your tooth come out," said Beth. "It's called Crunchy Lunchy!"

Luke liked the sound of this plan. "All right," he said. "I'll try it."

Beth took everyone to her house. She set the kitchen table. Then she put out all kinds of crunchy, chewy foods.

"This is how I lost my first tooth," she said. "I was eating this same lunch. I bit down hard, and my tooth came out. Ever since then, we've called this meal Crunchy Lunchy."

The four friends sat down at the table. They ate apples. They ate carrots. They ate bagels.

Luke made sure to bite down hard. He wiggled his tooth after every bite.

"How does your tooth feel now?" Beth asked.

Luke wiggled his tooth one last time. "It feels the same," he said sadly.

Just then Max gave a shout. "Hey! One of my teeth fell out." He held up a little white tooth.

Luke groaned. "Now you've lost seven, and I still haven't lost even one!"

The kids went back to the park.

"There must be some way to get your tooth to come out," Max said. "But I don't have another plan."

"Me either," said Beth.

"I know what you should do," said Lisa.

"What?" said Luke. "Tell me, please!"

"Forget about that tooth," said Lisa. "That tooth has a plan of its own. It will fall out when it's ready."

And that's just what happened!

Reading with Your Child

Even though your child is reading more independently now, it is vital that you continue to take part in this important learning experience.

- Try to read with your child at least twenty minutes each day, as part of your regular routine.
- Encourage your child to keep favorite books in one convenient, cozy spot, so you don't waste valuable reading time looking for them.
- Read and familiarize yourself with the Phonic Guidelines on the next pages.
- Praise your young reader. Be the cheerleader, not the teacher. Your enthusiasm and encouragement are key ingredients in your child's success.

What to Do if Your Child Gets Stuck on a Word

- Wait a moment to see if he or she works it out alone.
- Help him or her decode the word phonetically. Say, "Try to sound it out."
- Encourage him or her to use picture clues. Say, "What does the picture show?"
- Encourage him or her to use context clues. Say, "What would make sense?"
- Ask him or her to try again. Say, "Read the sentence again and start the tricky word. Get your mouth ready to say it."
- If your child still doesn't "get" the word, tell him or her what it is. Don't wait for frustration to build.

What to Do if Your Child Makes a Mistake

- If the mistake makes sense, ignore it—unless it is part of a pattern of errors you wish to correct.
- If the mistake doesn't make sense, wait a moment to see if your child corrects it.
- If your child doesn't correct the mistake, ask him or her to try again, either by decoding the word or by using context or picture clues. Say, "Get your mouth ready" or "Make it sound right" or "Make it make sense."
- If your child still doesn't "get" the word, tell him or her what it is. Don't wait for frustration to build.

Phonic Guidelines

Use the following guidelines to help your child read the words in this story.

Short Vowels

When two consonants surround a vowel, the sound of the vowel is usually short. This means you pronounce *a* as in apple, *e* as in egg, *i* as in igloo, *o* as in octopus, and *u* as in umbrella. Words with short vowels include: *bed, big, box, cat, cup, dad, dog, get, hid, hop, hum, jam, kid, mad, met, mom, pen, ran, sad, sit, sun, top.*

R-Controlled Vowels

When a vowel is followed by the letter *r*, its sound is changed by the *r*. Words with *r*-controlled vowels include: *card, curl, dirt, farm, girl, herd, horn, jerk, torn, turn.*

Long Vowel and Silent E

If a word has a vowel followed by a consonant and an *e*, usually the vowel is long and the *e* is silent. Long vowels are pronounced the same way as their alphabet names. Words with a long vowel and silent *e* include: *bake, cute, dive, game, home, kite, mule, page, pole, ride, vote.*

Double Vowels

When two vowels are side by side, usually the first vowel is long and the second vowel is silent. Words with double vowels include: *boat, clean, gray, loaf, meet, neat, paint, pie, play, rain, sleep, tried.*

Diphthongs

Sometimes when two vowels (or a vowel and a consonant) are side by side, they combine to make a diphthong—a sound that is different from long or short vowel sounds. Diphthongs are: *au/aw, ew, oi/oy, ou/ow.* Words with diphthongs include: *auto, brown, claw, flew, found, join, toy.*

Double Consonants

When two identical consonants appear side by side, one of them is silent. Words with double consonants include: *bell, fuss, mess, mitt, puff, tall, yell.*

Consonant Blends

When two or more different consonants are side by side, they usually blend to make a combined sound. Words with consonant blends include: *bent, blob, bride, club, crib, drop, flip, frog, gift, glare, grip, help, jump, mask, most, pink, plane, ring, send, skate, sled, spin, steep, swim, trap, twin.*

Consonant Digraphs

Sometimes when two different consonants are side by side, they make a digraph that represents a single new sound. Consonant digraphs are: *ch, sh, th, wh*. Words with digraphs include: *bath, chest, lunch, sheet, think, whip, wish*.

Silent Consonants

Sometimes when two different consonants are side by side, one of them is silent. Words with silent consonants include: *back, dumb, knit, knot, lamb, sock, walk, wrap, wreck*.

Sight Words

Sight words are those words that a reader must learn to recognize immediately—by sight—instead of by sounding them out. They occur with high frequency in easy texts. Sight words include: *a, am, an, and, as, at, be, big, but, can, come, do, for, get, give, have, he, her, his, I, in, is, it, just, like, look, make, my, new, no, not, now, old, one, out, play, put, red, run, said, see, she, so, some, soon, that, the, then, there, they, to, too, two, under, up, us, very, want, was, we, went, what, when, where, with, you*.

Exceptions to the "Rules"

Although much of the English language is phonically regular, there are many words that don't follow the above guidelines. For example, a particular combination of letters can represent more than one sound. Double *oo* can represent a long *oo* sound, as in words such as *boot, cool,* and *moon*; or it can represent a short *oo* sound, as in words such as *foot, good,* and *hook*. The letters *ow* can represent a diphthong, as in words such as *brow, fowl,* and *town*; or they can represent a long *o* sound, as in words such as *blow, snow,* and *tow*. Additionally, some high-frequency words such as *some, come, have,* and *said* do not follow the guidelines at all, and *ough* appears in such different-sounding words as *although, enough,* and *thought*.

The phonic guidelines provided in this book are just that—guidelines. They do not cover all the irregularities in our rich and varied language, but are intended to correspond roughly to the phonic lessons taught in the the first and second grades. Phonics provides the foundation for learning to read. Repetition, visual clues, context, and sheer experience provide the rest.